PLAYS FOR PERFORMANCE

*A series designed for
contemporary production and study
Edited by
Nicholas Rudall and Bernard Sahlins*

MOLIÈRE

The Bourgeois Gentleman

In a New Translation and Adaptation by
Bernard Sahlins

Ivan R. Dee
CHICAGO

Library of Congress Cataloging-in-Publication Data:
Molière, 1622–1673.
    [Bourgeois gentilhomme. English]
    The bourgeois gentleman / Molière ; in a new translation and adaptation by Bernard Sahlins.
        p. cm. — (Plays for performance)
    ISBN 1-56663-303-6 (cloth : alk. paper) —
ISBN 1-56663-304-4 (pbk : alk. paper)
    I. Sahlins, Bernard. II. Title. III. Series.
PQ1829.A48 2000
842'.4—dc21   00-020882

INTRODUCTION

by Bernard Sahlins

Molière (Jean-Baptiste Poquelin, 1622–1673) stands as an Olympian peak in the long march of comedy from Menander, through the Roman mime, to the commedia dell'arte, to the film and stage comedies of today. His plays remain loved, popular, and frequently performed. Why? Not because he knew how to make a joke, or because he was a most skilled inventor of comic situations. He surely was masterful in these areas, but they were not the essence of his lasting appeal. What accounts for his survival was the brilliant employment of these talents in the service of character rather than gags, of behavior rather than comment. While he dealt with the pretensions of misanthropes and misers and social strivers, it was his special art to make them real people, and to teach us to understand our own potential for being misanthropes or misers or social strivers. Thus it is for his characters and their richly comical dilemmas that we continue to appreciate Molière. He was no revolutionary nor, in the narrow sense, a political animal. He saw clearly, comically, and humanly.

The Bourgeois Gentleman was written in 1670, hastily, to the king's order, as a "divertemento," a comedy-ballet with music (by Jean-Baptiste Lully) and dancing. This was a fairly common form, forerunner of today's musical comedies. It conventionally mandated a masquerade as the closing section. Given its hasty composition and the restrictions of its conventions, one could hardly expect a tightly plotted piece featuring profound character development. And, true enough, the play is structurally weak. This is no farce with accelerating plot complications, no well-made play with calculated plot dynamics; rather it is closer to cabaret, to a series of comic sketches, but its popularity over the years—the art of it—lies in its rich comic invention and its sure delineation of character.

Molère's century witnessed an accelerating rise of the middle class. Many of its members were entering the king's service, many growing rich, and their pretensions, well encapsulated in our play's title, were a ripe target for comedy. But Molière, ever the courageous boundary pusher, was evenhanded in his choice of targets. M. Jourdain is no less avaricious than the play's swindling nobleman. Indeed, by contrast to the nobleman's greed for money, Jourdain's greed for learning and acceptance is at times almost touching.

That the appeal of *The Bourgeois Gentleman* is far-flung, beyond the seventeenth century and beyond the borders of France, is evident by the fact that translations exist in close to fifty languages. None of the characters, major or minor, has dated. Most of the comedy still appeals. And the underlying themes of social striving, financial greed, and love's ingenuity are as relevant as when the play was written.

Since the play was written as a musical, it would be a most worthy project to mount a production that included singers, musicians, and dancers. Clearly present-day theatre economics would make this possible only on the nonprofessional stage. In the hope of encouraging a school production of this magnitude, I have outlined some suggestions for dances to accompany the work. These are indicated throughout the text in brackets.

CHARACTERS

MONSIEUR JOURDAIN, the would-be gentleman
MADAME JOURDAIN, his wife
LUCILE, their daughter
NICOLE, servant to Madame Jourdain
CLÉONTE, Lucile's suitor
COVIELLE, servant to Cléonte
DORANTE, a nobleman
DORIMÈNE, a countess
MUSIC MASTER
DANCE MASTER
FENCING MASTER
PHILOSOPHER
TAILOR
TAILOR'S APPRENTICE
SERVANTS
MUFTI
Music and Dance Students, Tailors and Cooks,
Singers and Dancers, Notary

The Bourgeois Gentleman

[We start with a ballet. Monsieur Jourdain, attempting to learn to dance. He is amiable, earnest, and willing, but hopelessly untalented. During the ballet a series of projections. The front page of a newspaper: The French Gazette *with the date, January 6, 1669, and the headline,* M. JOURDAIN, EX-STREET CLEANER, NOW THE RICHEST MAN IN FRANCE. *A drawing of Jourdain accompanies the article. The dates and headlines change: February 14, 1669,* M. JOURDAIN'S PRIMARY SCHOOL TEACHER: "HE DIDN'T READ VERY WELL, BUT HE WAS VERY GOOD AT NUMBERS." *August 20, 1669,* M. JOURDAIN . . . *etc. The ballet ends.]*

A young Music Student at a table in the Jourdain sitting room. He is composing, singing as he writes, and doing all the parts from bass to soprano in appropriate registers.

Enter the Music Master, two Musicians, the Dance Master, four Dancers. The two mincing masters are outwardly cordial with each other though they are rivals.

MUSIC MASTER: *(to musicians)* Come in, come in. We'll wait here for him.

DANCE MASTER: *(to dancers)* Dancers this way.

MUSIC MASTER: *(crossing to the music student)* Finished?

STUDENT: Yes. *(handing him the music sheet)*

MUSIC MASTER: Let's see. *(he vocalizes a few bars running through all the registers)* Very good.

DANCE MASTER: A new piece?

MUSIC MASTER: Yes, a serenade. I set him working on it while we wait for our "gentleman" to wake up.

DANCE MASTER: May I see it?

MUSIC MASTER: You shall hear it when *he* decides to show up. He's been dressing for an hour.

DANCE MASTER: *(looking around, appreciatively)* Still, you and I have done well for ourselves.

MUSIC MASTER: Yes, indeed. A nice source of income for us, this simple Monsieur Jourdain, with those visions of rank and status running around in his head. It would be a good thing for dance *and* music if everybody were like him.

DANCE MASTER: Up to a point. I'd be happier if he really understood the beauty of what we offer him.

MUSIC MASTER: Ah, true—but he pays well. And that's what the arts need nowadays.

DANCE MASTER: I admit it. I enjoy recognition. Applause excites me, challenges me. But playing for morons and listening to their stupid comments is torture. The real pleasure—may I just finish—comes from performing for people who recognize the subtle beauty of my work and who give me their warm approval. Nothing is more exquisitely rewarding than enlightened praise.

MUSIC MASTER: But it doesn't pay the rent. Solid praise accompanied by solid cash is what we need. Now it's true our "gentleman" is a . . . bit limited. He has an opinion about everything and knows nothing. He is generous with applause—but it's always at the wrong time. Still, I find his taste is refined by his money. His purse is filled with wonderful judgments. His praise is golden.

DANCE MASTER: There's some truth in that, but money isn't everything. A true artist demeans himself by chasing after it.

MUSIC MASTER: Hmm. I haven't seen you refuse our man's cash.

DANCE MASTER: True. But for me it's not all-important, and I still wish his taste was as sound as his money.

MUSIC MASTER: I'm with you. But it's a fair trade. We try to enlighten him, he helps our careers. We get to show our work, he pays for it.

(Enter Jourdain and two servants. Jourdain is wearing a dressing gown and a nightcap.)

JOURDAIN: Ah, gentlemen. Great to see you. Ready to show me your little piece?

DANCE MASTER: Excuse me?

JOURDAIN: You know . . . what do you call it . . . your prologue . . . dialogue . . . your show. . . . You know . . . a little song, a little dance . . . some . . .

MUSIC MASTER: We await your pleasure.

JOURDAIN: Oh. Sorry I've held you up, but today I get my new suit—the latest court style—and my damned tailor sent me some silk stockings that are so tight I thought I'd never get them on. . . .

MUSIC MASTER: We're here to serve at your convenience.

JOURDAIN: I want you both to stay until they've brought me my clothes so you can see what a real gentleman is wearing these days.

DANCE MASTER: As you wish.

13

JOURDAIN: You'll see me dressed from head to foot in the height of fashion. . . .

MUSIC MASTER: We can't wait.

JOURDAIN: Meanwhile I had this dressing gown made for me. . . .

DANCE MASTER: Divine.

JOURDAIN: My tailor tells me that classy people wear this in the morning. . . .

MUSIC MASTER: It becomes you.

JOURDAIN: Valet!

FIRST SERVANT: What can I do for you, sir?

JOURDAIN: Nothing. Just checking to see if you were paying attention. *(to the Masters)* I love having servants. What do you think of their uniforms?

DANCE MASTER: Magnificent.

JOURDAIN: *(opens his dressing gown to show tight red velvet breeches and a short green velvet jacket)* This is what I wear for my morning exercises.

MUSIC MASTER: Utterly charming.

JOURDAIN: Boy!

FIRST SERVANT: Yes, sir.

JOURDAIN: The other boy.

SECOND SERVANT: Yes, sir.

JOURDAIN: Hold my gown. *(hands off his dressing gown; preens)* What do you think?

DANCE MASTER: Perfect. Couldn't be better.

JOURDAIN: Good. Now let's tend to your little business.

MUSIC MASTER: First, I'd like you to hear a serenade which this young man *(points to student)* has composed for you. He's one of my pupils. Very gifted.

JOURDAIN: Pupil? You too good for this job?

MUSIC MASTER: Don't let the word pupil put you off, sir. Gifted pupils often know as much as the greatest masters. The melody is as lovely as it can be. Just listen.

JOURDAIN: Give me my dressing gown so I can hear this properly . . . wait, I think it will be better without the dressing gown. . . . No, give it back to me. That will be best.

A SINGER: *(or the pupil)* Night and day for you I pine,
By your fair eyes laid low.
If you thus treat one who loves you so,
What happens to your foe?

JOURDAIN: Sounds depressing to me. Could you lighten it up a little?

MUSIC MASTER: The melody, sir, must fit the mood of the words.

JOURDAIN: I knew a song once . . . very pretty . . . wait a minute . . . hmm . . . now, how does it go?

MUSIC MASTER: I have no idea.

JOURDAIN: There's a sheep in it.

MUSIC MASTER: A sheep?

JOURDAIN: Yes. Ah, I have it. *(he sings)*
I thought my dear Jenny
Was sweeter than any.
I thought my dear Jenny
Was mild as a lamb.

15

But the truth is not pretty,
She's cruel and quite petty,
That mildness was only a sham

JOURDAIN: Now isn't that pretty?

MUSIC MASTER: Prettiest I ever heard.

DANCE MASTER: You sing it so beautifully.

JOURDAIN: And I never studied music!

MUSIC MASTER: You should—since you're learning to dance. The two arts go together.

JOURDAIN: Do society people study music too?

MUSIC MASTER: Yes, sir.

JOURDAIN: Then I will too. But I don't know where I'll find the time. There's not only my fencing lessons, I hired a philosophy professor. Starts this morning.

MUSIC MASTER: Philosophy is one thing, but music, sir, music . . .

DANCE MASTER: Music and dance. Music and dance are all you really need.

MUSIC MASTER: All people need music.

DANCE MASTER: All people need dance.

MUSIC MASTER: All the world's disorders, its wars, are caused by the absence of music.

DANCE MASTER: All the ills and sorrows of mankind, all the fatal misfortunes which fill the pages of history—the political blunders, the mistakes made by great generals—all come from the absence of dance.

JOURDAIN: Really? Why is that?

MUSIC MASTER: Isn't war caused by a lack of harmony between men?

JOURDAIN: By God, it is.

MUSIC MASTER: If all men learned music, wouldn't the result be harmony, and therefore universal peace?

JOURDAIN: You're absolutely right!

DANCE MASTER: And when a man has made a mistake in his family affairs or in government or in the military, don't we always say, "So and so has made a false step?"

JOURDAIN: We do say that, don't we?

DANCE MASTER: And what causes a false step but not knowing how to dance?

JOURDAIN: That's true. You're both right.

MUSIC MASTER: Now, may we show you our production?

JOURDAIN: Yes. Yes.

MUSIC MASTER: *(signaling the singers to come forward)* Now imagine they are dressed as shepherds.

JOURDAIN: Shepherds! Why is it always shepherds? All I ever see in these things is shepherds. What about mermaids?

MUSIC MASTER: When people communicate musically, for the sake of authenticity, we put them in a pastoral setting. Shepherds are always singing. It's not natural for the nobility or commoners—or mermaids—to sing their dialogue.

JOURDAIN: All right. Let's hear the thing.

DANCE MASTER: And as my part of the performance, our dancers will display the versatility and beauty afforded by dance.

JOURDAIN: More shepherds?

DANCE MASTER: Whatever you please.

(the singers and dancers perform)

WOMAN: Love is a torturing tyrant
That fills the heart with strife.
Give way to sighs and rapture,
Give up liberty and life.

MAN 1: Nothing's so sweet as loving,
Two hearts join in a kiss.
Happiness comes with caring,
To lose love is to lose bliss.

MAN 2: I long to be in love,
But a truth I must confess.
I've sought but cannot find
A faithful shepherdess.
Women are fickle and untrue ever,
I give up love now and forever.

MAN 1: Love is so sweet.

WOMAN: Freedom is sweeter.

MAN 2: Love is a cheat.

MAN 1: My darling, my sweet.

WOMAN: *(to Man 2)* Dear love, I adore you.

MAN 2: My dear, I abhor you.

MAN 1 TO MAN 2: Learn to love. And you will see . . .

WOMAN: Your shepherdess will faithful be.

MAN 2: Faithful! This I'd like to see.

WOMAN: *(to Man 2)* To prove a woman can be true
I offer here my heart to you.

MAN 2: But shepherdess how can I know
That what you say is true?

WOMAN: Let us test if it be so,
You trust me and I'll trust you.

MAN 2: And punished by the gods shall be
The first to fail in constancy.

THE THREE SINGERS: Such noble feelings lift our
hearts
And give us hope that love survives.
How sweet is love in all its parts,
These two will ever share their lives.

JOURDAIN: Is it over?

MUSIC MASTER: Yes.

JOURDAIN: Well, a very neat job. Some parts of it
were pretty good.

(exit dancers and singers)

DANCE MASTER: That was just a taste of the little ballet we've organized for you.

JOURDAIN: Well, it's to be ready this afternoon. The
special lady I've ordered it for is honoring me by
dining here today.

DANCE MASTER: It's all ready.

MUSIC MASTER: But sir, this is not enough. A person
like you who lives so well and with a taste for the
finer things in life should have a musicale at
home every Wednesday or Thursday.

JOURDAIN: Do society people have that?

MUSIC MASTER: Yes, sir.

JOURDAIN: Then I'll have it. It will be nice?

MUSIC MASTER: Very nice. You'll need three voices: soprano, counter-tenor, and bass: accompanied by bass viol, lute, and harpsichord for continuo, plus two violins for melody.

JOURDAIN: You must have an accordion. Now that's an instrument I like. Full of harmony.

MUSIC MASTER: Just leave all that to us.

JOURDAIN: Anyway, don't forget to send me some singers to entertain at the meal.

MUSIC MASTER: You'll have everything you need.

JOURDAIN: Above all, make sure we have a nice ballet.

DANCE MASTER: I'm sure you'll be very pleased, especially with the brilliant minuet.

JOURDAIN: Minuet! That's my dance! You must see me do it. Come on, professor.

DANCE MASTER: A hat, sir, if you please. One does not dance the minuet without a hat. *(Jourdain takes a servant's hat and claps it on his nightcap. The Dance Master takes him by both hands and sings the melody of a minuet.)* La, la, la; La, la, la, la, la, la. La, la, la, repeat. La, la, la; La, la. Keep in time, please. La, la, la, la. Now the right leg, la, la, la, don't shake your shoulders quite so much. La, la, la, la, la; La, la, la, la, la. Both arms are stiff—are they crippled? La, la, la, la, la. Hold your head higher—turn out your toes. La, la, la. Stand up straight . . .

JOURDAIN: That's a lot of things to do!

DANCE MASTER: Superb. Beautifully danced.

JOURDAIN: Ah! I just remembered. Teach me how to bow to a countess. I'll need to know soon.

DANCE MASTER: A bow to a countess?

JOURDAIN: Yes, her name is Dorimène.

DANCE MASTER: Give me your hand.

JOURDAIN: No, you do it alone. I'll remember.

DANCE MASTER: If you want to show the greatest respect, you make your first bow while stepping backward, then three bows while stepping forward, bending down to her knees at the last one.

JOURDAIN: Show me. *(the Dance Master demonstrates)* Good. That's enough.

(enter a Servant)

SERVANT: Sir, your fencing master is on his way in.

JOURDAIN: Good. I'll have my lesson now. *(exit Servant)* You two, watch this.

(He mimes feints and parries. Enter Fencing Master and Servant carrying two foils. The Master takes one of the foils and hands the other to Jourdain.)

FENCING MASTER: Now, sir, your salute. Body straight. A little more weight on the left thigh. The legs not so far apart. The feet on the same line. Wrist in a line with your thigh. The point of your foil in line with your shoulder. The arm not quite so extended. The left hand at eye level. The left shoulder back a little more. Head up. The look firm. Advance . . . keep the body rigid. . . . Engage my foil on quart and follow through. One, two. . . . Recover. . . . Again. . . . Feet firm. . . . One, two. . . . Retreat. . . . When you attack, sir, it's foil first with the body well back and sideways. . . . One, two,

engage my foil in tierce and follow through. . . .
Advance . . . the body steady. . . . Advance . . . one,
two. . . . Now from that position. One two. . . .
Recover. . . . Once more. . . . One, two. . . . Retreat. . . . On guard, sir, on guard.

(the Fencing Master delivers two or three hits)

JOURDAIN: Ugh! Hey!

MUSIC MASTER: You're doing beautifully.

FENCING MASTER: As I've told you, the whole art of
fencing consists of two things: hitting and not
being hit. And as I proved the other day with
demonstrative logic, it's impossible for you to be
hit if you divert your opponent's weapon from
the line of your body. You do that with a simple
twist of the wrist, either inward or outward.

JOURDAIN: So, by demonstrative logic, even a coward
can be sure of killing his man and not getting
killed?

FENCING MASTER: Exactly. Didn't you just see that
demonstrated?

JOURDAIN: Yes.

FENCING MASTER: So you see why the state should
value us so highly and how superior is the art of
fencing to such useless arts as dancing, music . . .

DANCE MASTER: Hold on there, Monsieur Fencer,
show some respect for the art of dancing.

MUSIC MASTER: And, if you please, a little more ap-
preciation for music.

FENCING MASTER: You are a ludicrous pair—compar-
ing your arts with mine.

MUSIC MASTER: Well, aren't you a big, important man.

DANCE MASTER: This ridiculous aberration with his padded chest.

FENCING MASTER: Steady, little dancer, I can make you hop to my tune till you beg. As for you, my midget musician, one thrust and you'll be singing in a very high key.

DANCE MASTER: I, Monsieur Hardware, will teach you your own trade.

JOURDAIN: Are you crazy, picking a fight with a man who knows all about tierce and quart and can kill people by demonstrative logic?

DANCE MASTER: I don't give a damn for his demonstrative logic *or* his tierce and quart.

JOURDAIN: I'd go easy if I were you.

FENCING MASTER: *(to Dance Master)* What! You impudent fop.

JOURDAIN: Please, gentlemen . . . peace.

DANCE MASTER: You're a dumb, clumsy bull.

FENCING MASTER: If I let myself go . . .

JOURDAIN: Calm. I appeal for calm.

DANCE MASTER: I'll tango on your face . . .

JOURDAIN: Please!

FENCING MASTER: I'll slice you like a salami.

JOURDAIN: Oh, dear!

MUSIC MASTER: Teach the beast some manners.

JOURDAIN: Now, don't you start.

(enter the Philosopher)

JOURDAIN: Thank heaven, Monsieur Philosopher. The nick of time. Use your philosophy to make peace here.

PHILOSOPHER: What is the essence of your problem, gentlemen?

JOURDAIN: They are in such a rage about which has the noblest profession, they are ready to fight. And the language!

PHILOSOPHER: Shame, gentlemen. Should a man so lose self-control? Haven't you read Seneca's learned treatise on anger? Is there anything more base and shameful, he asks, than that passion which turns a man into a savage beast? Should not reason be the mistress of our actions?

DANCE MASTER: Sir, without provocation, this ass insults us by sneering at dancing and music.

PHILOSOPHER: A wise man stands above insults. The best response to calumny is equanimity and patience.

FENCING MASTER: These two had the audacity to equate their degenerate professions with my ancient, manly art.

PHILOSOPHER: Should this offend you? Men should not quarrel over position and precedence. What truly distinguishes one man from another is wisdom and virtue.

DANCE MASTER: Dancing is the supreme art.

MUSIC MASTER: Music has been revered throughout history.

FENCING MASTER: Hah! Fencing reigns.

PHILOSOPHER: Then where do you put philosophy? I think the three of you are arrogant and impudent men to give the name of high art to matters which barely rise to the level of craft in common with the wretched trades of gladiator, minstrel, and posturer.

FENCING MASTER: Up yours, philosopher.

MUSIC MASTER: Get out, you threadbare pedant.

DANCE MASTER: You crackbrain professor.

PHILOSOPHER: What! You ignorant churls . . . I'm a Ph.D.! *(he attacks the other three who unite to beat him)*

JOURDAIN: Monsieur Philosopher!

PHILOSOPHER: Villains! Varlots! Impudent scoundrels!

JOURDAIN: Monsieur Philosopher!

DANCE MASTER: A plague on this jackass!

JOURDAIN: Gentlemen, please!

PHILOSOPHER: Beasts!

JOURDAIN: Monsieur Philosopher!

MUSIC MASTER: To hell with him and his pretentious nonsense.

PHILOSOPHER: Thieves, vagabonds, rogues, imposters!

JOURDAIN: Monsieur Philosopher. Gentlemen. Monsieur Philosopher. Gentlemen. Monsieur Philosopher.

(they exit, fighting)

JOURDAIN: Well, fight all you like. There's nothing I can do about it. I won't soil my dressing gown to separate you. I'd be crazy to get in the middle of that. I could get hurt!

(enter the Philosopher, tidying his clothing)

PHILOSOPHER: Now, let's have our lesson.

JOURDAIN: I'm sorry you were hit.

PHILOSOPHER: It's nothing. A true philosopher knows how to deal with reality. I shall write a satire against them in the style of Juvenal. That will destroy them. Yes! Now let's drop the matter. What do you want to learn?

JOURDAIN: Everything. Above all I want knowledge. I'm furious that my mother and father didn't make me study when I was young.

PHILOSOPHER: That's a very commendable sentiment. *Nam sine doctrina vita est quasi imago.* You understand . . . you know Latin, of course.

JOURDAIN: Of course, but let's just pretend I don't.

PHILOSOPHER: "Without knowledge, life is close to an imitation of death."

JOURDAIN: That Latin knows what it's talking about.

PHILOSOPHER: You do have some schooling in the basic elements of knowledge?

JOURDAIN: Oh, yes, I can read and write.

PHILOSOPHER: Where would you like to begin? How about logic?

JOURDAIN: Sure. What is it?

PHILOSOPHER: The science that teaches the three laws of reason.

JOURDAIN: What are the three laws of reason?

PHILOSOPHER: The first, the second, and the third.

JOURDAIN: Got it.

PHILOSOPHER: The first is to formulate properly by means of universals. The second is to analyze properly by means of categories. And the third, to deduce properly by means of such examples as Barbara, Celarent, Darii, Ferio, Baralipton, and so forth.

JOURDAIN: Ugh! I don't like this logic. Let's learn something prettier.

PHILOSOPHER: How about ethics?

JOURDAIN: Ethics?

PHILOSOPHER: Yes.

JOURDAIN: What do they do?

PHILOSOPHER: It teaches morality and the control of the passions.

JOURDAIN: No, none of that. I have a temper, and when I want to get mad, I want to get good and mad.

PHILOSOPHER: How about physics?

JOURDAIN: What has this physics to say for itself?

PHILOSOPHER: Physics is the science that explains the principles of natural phenomena and the properties of matter. It deals with the nature of elements, of metals, minerals, stones, plants, and animals, and teaches us the causes of meteors,

27

rainbows, St. Elmo's fire, comets, lightning, thunder, thunderbolts, rain, snow, hail, winds, and whirlwinds.

JOURDAIN: La-di-da. La-di-da. Too much content.

PHILOSOPHER: Well then, what would you like me to teach you?

JOURDAIN: How about spelling?

PHILOSOPHER: Gladly. Let us begin with a precise explanation of the nature of letters and of the different way in which each is pronounced. First I must tell you that the letters are divided into vowels, so-called because they express the sounds of the voice, and consonants, so-called because they sound with the vowels. There are five vowels, or voices: "A, E, I, O, U."

JOURDAIN: No!

PHILOSOPHER: The vowel "A" is formed by opening the mouth wide. Ah.

JOURDAIN: Ah. Ah. Yes.

PHILOSOPHER: The vowel "E" is formed by moving the lower jaw closer to the upper jaw. E.

JOURDAIN: Ah, E. Ah, E. Yes, you're right. How beautiful it is.

PHILOSOPHER: The vowel "I" is made by opening the mouth as far as possible. Ah, E, I.

JOURDAIN: Ah, E, I, I, I. It's true. Three cheers for philosophy.

PHILOSOPHER: The vowel "O" is formed by opening the jaws and bringing the corners of the mouth close together. O.

JOURDAIN: O, O. Nothing could be truer. Ah, E, I, O, E, O. That's wonderful. E, O. E, O. *(traditionally the actor here is imitating a donkey braying)*

PHILOSOPHER: The opening of the mouth forms a little circle which represents the "O."

JOURDAIN: O. O. O. You're right. O. Oh what a fine thing it is to know something.

PHILOSOPHER: The vowel "U" is formed by bringing the teeth close together without quite touching and extending the lips at the same time, making a small opening. U.

JOURDAIN: U. U. Absolutely correct.

PHILOSOPHER: The lips are extended as if you were pouting, so if you want to express contempt for someone, all you say to him is U.

JOURDAIN: U. U. That's right. Oh, why didn't I start studying sooner. I'd know all that.

PHILOSOPHER: Tomorrow we will consider the other letters: the consonants.

JOURDAIN: Are they as complicated as these vowels?

PHILOSOPHER: Certainly. For instance, the consonant "D" is pronounced by striking the tip of the tongue just above the upper teeth. D.

JOURDAIN: D. D. Oh yes! What wonders.

PHILOSOPHER: The "F" by resting the upper teeth on the lower lip. F.

JOURDAIN: F. F. Absolutely true. Oh! Father and mother, this is your fault.

PHILOSOPHER: And the "R" by placing the tip of the tongue against the roof of the mouth, yielding to

a forceful rush of air from behind, then return-
ing to the same place over and over. Rrrrr . . .

JOURDAIN: R. R. Ra. Rrrrrrrah. That's right. What a
clever man you are, and how much time I've lost.
Rrrrrah.

PHILOSOPHER: I will explain these important phenomena to you in great detail.

JOURDAIN: Oh! Please do. Now I must take you into
my confidence. I'm in love with a person of very
high rank, and I'd appreciate your help in writing
a little love note.

PHILOSOPHER: Of course.

JOURDAIN: It should be in a noble style . . .

PHILOSOPHER: No question. Would you like it to be
in verse?

JOURDAIN: No. No. None of that poetic stuff.

PHILOSOPHER: You want just prose.

JOURDAIN: No, I don't want prose either.

PHILOSOPHER: It must be one or the other.

JOURDAIN: Why?

PHILOSOPHER: Because, sir, our only means of expression are poetry or prose.

JOURDAIN: There is nothing but prose or poetry?

PHILOSOPHER: No, sir. All that is not prose is poetry,
and all that is not poetry is prose.

JOURDAIN: And when we speak, like now, what is
that?

PHILOSOPHER: Prose.

JOURDAIN: When I say, "Nicole, bring me my slippers," that's prose?

PHILOSOPHER: Yes, it is.

JOURDAIN: My God! I've been speaking prose for over forty years and didn't even know it. I'm in your debt for telling me this. Now I want to put in my note, "Fair Countess, your matchless eyes make me die of love." But I'd like this put in noble style, prettily said.

PHILOSOPHER: Say that the fire of her eyes reduces your heart to ashes, that night and day, because of her, you suffer the tortures . . .

JOURDAIN: No, no, no. I don't want any of that. I just want what I told you: "Fair Countess. Your matchless eyes make me die of love," but elegant.

PHILOSOPHER: You might amplify that a bit.

JOURDAIN: No amplify. I just want those very words in the note, but arranged in a fashionable way. Just take me through some of the different ways they can be put.

PHILOSOPHER: You can, first of all, put them as you had them, "Fair Countess, your matchless eyes make me die of love." Or else: "Of love, fair Countess, your matchless eyes make me die." Or else: "Your eyes, matchless, of love, Countess fair, make me die." Or else: "Die, fair Countess, of love, your matchless eyes me make." Or else: "Me, your matchless eyes of love make die, fair Countess."

JOURDAIN: Of all of those, which is best?

PHILOSOPHER: The way you said it. "Fair Countess, your matchless eyes make me die of love."

31

JOURDAIN: Amazing! I've never studied, but I did it on the first try. I thank you with all my heart. Please come again tomorrow—early.

PHILOSOPHER: Without fail.

(exit Philosopher)

JOURDAIN: *(to his servants)* Don't tell me my gaddamned new suit isn't here.

SERVANT: No, sir.

JOURDAIN: That pimp of a tailor makes me wait on a day like this when I'm so busy. I am furious. May he succumb to fever, that tailor. To the devil with that tailor. May he writhe with plague, that tailor. If I had him here right now, that dog of a tailor, that pig of a tailor, I would . . .

(enter Tailor and Apprentice carrying Jourdain's suit)

JOURDAIN: Oh there you are. I was just about to get angry with you.

TAILOR: I couldn't get here any sooner. I had twenty seamstresses working on your suit.

JOURDAIN: The silk stockings you sent were so tight I could hardly get them on. Broke two stitches already. And the shoes you made me pinch unbearably.

TAILOR: Not at all, sir.

JOURDAIN: What, not at all?

TAILOR: They do not pinch at all.

JOURDAIN: I tell you they pinch.

TAILOR: You imagine it.

JOURDAIN: I imagine it because I feel it. What kind of talk is that?

TAILOR: *(holding up suit)* Look at that! You won't find a finer, more beautifully designed suit at the court itself. It's a masterpiece. To have invented a suit that's formal without being black. The most skilled tailors couldn't equal it in half a dozen tries.

JOURDAIN: What's this? You've put the fleur-de-lys upside down!

TAILOR: You never told me you wanted them right side up.

JOURDAIN: Did I have to tell you that?

TAILOR: Of course. All refined people wear them this way.

JOURDAIN: Refined people wear the fleur-de-lys upside down?

TAILOR: Yes, sir.

JOURDAIN: Oh? That's all right then.

TAILOR: If you prefer I can put them the other way.

JOURDAIN: No, no.

TAILOR: Just say the word . . .

JOURDAIN: No, I tell you. It's fine. Do you think the suit will suit me?

TAILOR: Without question. I defy the greatest artist to paint a better match. I have a tailor who is a genius at pants and another who is the hero of our age at cutting a doublet.

JOURDAIN: The wig and the feathers—are they all right?

TAILOR: Everything is perfect.

JOURDAIN: *(peering at the coat the tailor himself is wearing)* Isn't that the same material you used on the last coat you made me?

TAILOR: You looked so handsome in it, I had to use it for myself.

JOURDAIN: I paid for that material.

TAILOR: Would you like to try on your suit?

JOURDAIN: Yes, hand it over.

TAILOR: Hold on. Let's do this properly. I've brought some men to dress you to music. Clothes like this require ceremony.

[Ballet. The Tailor claps his hands. Four Tailors accompanied by musicians now dress Jourdain in dance. It ends up with him showing off his new suit, asking for approval.]

APPRENTICE: Noble Sir, a tip for the tailors?

JOURDAIN: What did you call me?

APPRENTICE: Noble Sir.

JOURDAIN: "Noble Sir." That's what comes from dressing like a gentleman. Go through life dressed like a workman and no one will say, "Noble Sir." *(distributes money to tailors)* Here, that's for "Noble Sir."

APPRENTICE: My Lord, we are very much obliged to you.

JOURDAIN: "My Lord"! Oh, oh, "My Lord"! Wait, my friend, "My Lord" deserves a little something. There, that's what His Lordship gives you.

APPRENTICE: My Lord, we shall all drink to the health of Your Grace.

JOURDAIN: "Your Grace"! Oh! Oh! Oh! Wait, don't go. "Your Grace" to me! I swear if he goes as far as "Royal Highness," he'll empty my purse. There, that's for "Your Grace."

APPRENTICE: Sir, we thank you for your generosity.

JOURDAIN: A good thing he stopped. I was ready to give everything away.

(the Tailor and his assistants dance off)

JOURDAIN: *(to his two servants)* I'm taking a little walk around town to show off my new clothes. I want you to walk closely behind me so everyone can see you belong to me.

SERVANTS: Yes, sir.

JOURDAIN: And call Nicole. I have some instructions . . . never mind, she's coming. *(enter Nicole)* Now Nicole . . .

NICOLE: Yes, sir?

JOURDAIN: Listen carefully.

NICOLE: *(laughing)* Hee, hee, hee, hee, hee.

JOURDAIN: What's so funny?

NICOLE: Hee, hee, hee, hee, hee.

JOURDAIN: What does this braying mean?

NICOLE: Ho, ho, ho. How funny you look. Hee, hee, hee.

JOURDAIN: What do you mean?

NICOLE: Oh, God. Ha, ha, ha, ha, ha.

JOURDAIN: Hussy. Are you making fun of me?

NICOLE: Oh no, sir. I'd never do that. Hee, hee, hee, hee.

JOURDAIN: I'll spank you if you don't stop laughing.

NICOLE: Sir, I can't help it. Hee, hee, hee, hee, hee. You look ridiculous.

JOURDAIN: Will you stop it?

NICOLE: Sir, I'm sorry. But you look so funny I can't stop laughing. Hee, hee.

JOURDAIN: I swear, if you laugh once more, I swear I'll give you the worst beating imaginable.

NICOLE: It's over, sir. I won't laugh anymore.

JOURDAIN: Make sure you don't. Now, this afternoon I want you to clean . . .

NICOLE: Hee, hee.

JOURDAIN: And clean thoroughly . . .

NICOLE: Hee, hee.

JOURDAIN: I say I want you to clean up the drawing room and . . .

NICOLE: Hee, hee.

JOURDAIN: What, again?

NICOLE: *(collapsing with laughter)* Sir, it's better if you beat me than if I try to stop laughing. Hee, hee, hee, hee, hee.

JOURDAIN: You're driving me crazy.

NICOLE: I'll blow up if I don't laugh. Hee. Hee. Hee.

JOURDAIN: Have you ever seen anything like this? Instead of obeying orders she laughs in my face.

NICOLE: What do you want me to do, sir?

JOURDAIN: I want you, hussy, to clean the house for the company that's due here any minute.

NICOLE: Oh goodness. That ends my laughing. Your company always makes such a mess around here, it's enough to kill my sense of humor.

JOURDAIN: So, for your convenience, I should shut my door to everybody?

NICOLE: At least to certain people.

(enter Madame Jourdain)

MADAME J: Now, here's a new folly: this, outfit of yours, my dear husband. Are you crazy, decking yourself out like that? Do you want the whole world laughing at you?

JOURDAIN: Madame, only fools will laugh at me.

MADAME J: Then the whole world's foolish. Everybody's been laughing at you for a long time.

JOURDAIN: And please tell me, dear wife, who is everybody?

MADAME J: Everybody is anybody who has any sense at all, which is more than you have. The kind of life you're leading is a scandal. I don't even recognize our own house. You've made every day carnival time around here. From early morning the house is filled with the ungodly noise of fiddlers and singers, making enough racket to disturb the whole neighborhood.

NICOLE: Madame is right. I can't keep the house clean anymore with all this gang of people you bring in. They pick up mud from every part of the city and bring it back here.

JOURDAIN: Shut up, Nicole. That's quite a tongue you have for a servant girl.

MADAME J: Nicole is right; she has more sense than you. I'd like to know why you need a dance master at your age.

NICOLE: Or that great hulk of a fencing master who stomps around so hard the whole house shakes and all the floor tiles loosen up.

JOURDAIN: Shut up, both of you.

MADAME J: You'll learn to dance about the time you get too old to walk.

NICOLE: You want to kill somebody with your foil before you die?

JOURDAIN: I said, shut up! You're both ignorant. You know nothing of what's socially important.

MADAME J: You'd be better off thinking of a suitable marriage for your daughter, now that she's old enough.

JOURDAIN: I'll think about that when the right match comes along. But in the meantime I'll think of learning the finer things in life.

NICOLE: On top of that, Madame, I heard he's got himself a philosopher.

JOURDAIN: That's true. I want to be an intellectual, able to talk with people of quality about . . . things.

MADAME J: Why don't you try going to school? You can get yourself whipped at the same time.

JOURDAIN: Why not? I would gladly be publicly whipped if I could know all they teach at school.

NICOLE: Oh sure. That would improve the shape of your legs.

JOURDAIN: You think so?

MADAME J: All that is very important for running this house.

JOURDAIN: You're right, it would. You both speak like morons, and I'm ashamed of your ignorance. *(to Madame Jourdain)* For instance, do you know what you're speaking at this moment?

MADAME J: Yes. I know what I'm speaking is very well spoken; and you should think about changing your ways.

JOURDAIN: I don't mean that. I'm asking what the words are that you are speaking now?

MADAME J: They are very sensible words, which is more than I can say about your conduct.

JOURDAIN: I'm not speaking about that. I ask you, what is it that I'm speaking to you, that I'm saying to you now?

MADAME J: Stuff and nonsense.

JOURDAIN: No! No! It isn't that. What are both of us saying, the language we are using at this minute?

MADAME J: Well?

JOURDAIN: What is it called?

MADAME J: Whatever you'd like to call it.

JOURDAIN: It's prose, ignorant woman.

MADAME J: Prose?

JOURDAIN: Yes, prose. Everything that is prose is not poetry, and everything that is not poetry is not prose. There! See how liberating it is to study? *(to Nicole)* You, do you know what you have to do to make a "U"?

NICOLE: Excuse me? . . .

JOURDAIN: What do you do when you make a "U"?

NICOLE: What?

JOURDAIN: Just say U, to see.

NICOLE: All right. U.

JOURDAIN: What did you do?

NICOLE: I said U.

JOURDAIN: Yes, but when you said U, what did you do?

NICOLE: I did what you told me.

JOURDAIN: It's tiring having to deal with dummies. You thrust your lips out, and you let the upper jaw fall to meet the lower jaw. U, you see? U. I make a face. U.

NICOLE: Very pretty.

MADAME J: Wonderful.

JOURDAIN: Oh, what you would say if you could see my O and D, D and F.

MADAME J: What is all this foolishness?

NICOLE: What does it cure you of?

JOURDAIN: Dealing with such ignorant people makes me sick.

MADAME J: You should kick out all those charlatans and their ridiculous nonsense.

NICOLE: Especially that hulk of a fencing master who fills the house with dust.

JOURDAIN: That fencing master gets under your skin, doesn't he? I'll show you, right now, how foolish you are. *(he summons the servant with the foils, takes one, and hands the other to Nicole)* Take this. Demonstrative logic. The line of the body. When you thrust in quart, just do this, and when you thrust in tierce, do this. That's the sure way not to be killed. Isn't it wonderful to be certain of safety when you fight someone? Now, thrust at me a little, just to see.

NICOLE: Well, then. *(she makes several thrusts and pricks him)*

JOURDAIN: Ho, hold on! Easy! Damn this woman.

NICOLE: You told me to thrust.

JOURDAIN: Yes, but you thrust in tierce before you thrust in quart, and you didn't have the patience to wait till I parried.

MADAME J: You're out of your mind, dear husband, with all these crazy notions. It's all happened since you decided to hang around with the nobility.

JOURDAIN: It shows a lot more judgment than hanging around with your riff-raff.

MADAME J: Oh really? Like the nice business you've done with that freeloading count you're so close to?

JOURDAIN: Quiet! Watch what you say. You don't have any idea of how important he is. Count Dorante is a great lord, highly respected at court. Why, he speaks to the king just the way I speak to you. Isn't it a great honor that such a person should be seen with me, that he comes to my house so often, that he calls me his dear friend and treats me as an equal? You'd never guess how kind he is to me, showing me such special affection in public that I'm often embarrassed.

MADAME J: Yes, he's very kind and affectionate to you—and he loves your money.

JOURDAIN: Well, isn't it an honor for me to lend money to a man of such rank? And can I do any less for a count who calls me his dear friend?

MADAME J: And in return you get . . . ?

JOURDAIN: Things that would astonish you if you knew about them

MADAME J: What things?

JOURDAIN: It's business. You wouldn't understand. It's enough that if I've lent him money, he will repay it, and soon.

MADAME J: Yes, you can be sure of that.

JOURDAIN: Absolutely. He gave me his word he would pay it back . . .

MADAME J: Yes and you can trust him—not to.

JOURDAIN: His word as a gentleman.

MADAME J: Nonsense.

JOURDAIN: Sh! Here he is.

MADAME J: That's the last straw. He probably needs more money. Just the sight of him ruins my appetite.

JOURDAIN: Shh, I tell you.

(enter Dorante)

DORANTE: My dear friend Jourdain, how are you today?

JOURDAIN: Very well, sir, and humbly at your service.

DORANTE: And Madame Jourdain, how is she doing?

MADAME J: Madame Jourdain is doing as well as she can.

DORANTE: I say, Monsieur Jourdain, that is a serious suit.

JOURDAIN: *(to the women)* You see.

DORANTE: It is certainly—exuberant. None of the young people at court can match it.

JOURDAIN: Really?

MADAME J: *(to Nicole)* He scratches him where it itches.

DORANTE: Turn around. Very stylish.

MADAME J: *(to Nicole)* As foolish behind as in front.

DORANTE: I swear, Monsieur Jourdain, I'm very glad to see you. You are the man I admire most in the world. Only this morning I was talking about you in the king's bedchamber.

43

JOURDAIN: You do me too much honor, sir. *(to Madame J)* In the king's bedchamber!

DORANTE: Come, put your hat back on.

JOURDAIN: Sir, I know the respect I owe you.

DORANTE: Please . . . put it on. Let there be no ceremony between us, please.

JOURDAIN: Sir, I am your humble servant.

DORANTE: I won't cover unless you do.

JOURDAIN: *(putting on his hat)* I'd rather be impolite than troublesome.

DORANTE: As you know, I owe you money.

MADAME J: *(aside)* Yes, we know that very well.

DORANTE: More than once you have made me a loan, always graciously and with great generosity.

JOURDAIN: Sir, you are too kind.

DORANTE: But I am pledged to repay what I borrow and to show my gratitude for the favors done to me.

JOURDAIN: I don't doubt it, sir.

DORANTE: I've come to settle our accounts.

JOURDAIN: *(to his wife)* See how wrong you were?

DORANTE: I resolved to pay you back promptly.

JOURDAIN: *(to his wife)* I told you so.

DORANTE: So shall we total it all up?

JOURDAIN: *(to his wife)* You and your ridiculous suspicions.

44

DORANTE: Do you remember exactly how much you've lent me?

JOURDAIN: I think so. I made a little note of it. Here it is. On one occasion, two hundred louis.

DORANTE: Correct.

JOURDAIN: Then one hundred and twenty.

DORANTE: Right.

JOURDAIN: Then one hundred and forty.

DORANTE: Yes.

JOURDAIN: Adding up to four hundred and sixty louis, or five thousand and sixty francs.

DORANTE: The accounting is absolutely correct. Five thousand and sixty francs.

JOURDAIN: One thousand eight hundred and thirty-two francs to your plume seller.

DORANTE: Exactly.

JOURDAIN: Two thousand seven hundred and eighty francs to your tailor.

DORANTE: True.

JOURDAIN: Four thousand three hundred seventy-nine francs, twelve sous, and eight farthings to your haberdasher.

DORANTE: Excellent. Twelve sous, eight farthings. Precision accounting.

JOURDAIN: And one thousand seven hundred forty-eight francs, seven sous, and four farthings to your saddler.

DORANTE: It's all correct. What's the total?

JOURDAIN: Total: fifteen thousand eight hundred francs.

DORANTE: The total is also correct. Now add the two thousand two hundred francs you are now going to lend me, and that will make exactly eighteen thousand which I will pay you at the earliest opportunity.

MADAME J: *(to Jourdain)* Well, didn't I guess it?

JOURDAIN: Quiet!

DORANTE: Will it be inconvenient to lend me that much?

JOURDAIN: No, no.

MADAME J: *(to Jourdain)* He's milking you like a cow.

JOURDAIN: Quiet!

DORANTE: If it's difficult for you, I'll get it somewhere else.

JOURDAIN: Oh no, sir.

MADAME J: He won't be satisfied until he ruins you.

JOURDAIN: I said, quiet!

DORANTE: If it's a problem for you, just say so.

JOURDAIN: Not at all, sir.

MADAME J: He's nothing but a swindler.

JOURDAIN: Be still.

DORANTE: There are plenty of people who would be glad to lend it to me, but since you're my best friend I thought it would be insulting if I asked anyone else.

JOURDAIN: You do me too much honor, sir. I will go and get what you want.

MADAME J: What! You're going to give him some more?

JOURDAIN: What can I do? Do you expect me to refuse a man of this rank who spoke about me this morning in the king's bedchamber?

MADAME J: Just go. You're nothing but a credulous fool.

(exit Jourdain)

DORANTE: You seem troubled, Madame Jourdain. Is something the matter?

MADAME J: I wasn't born yesterday. I'm old enough to see what's going on.

DORANTE: And your daughter? I haven't seen her.

MADAME J: My daughter is fine where she is.

DORANTE: How is she getting along?

MADAME J: On her two legs.

DORANTE: Wouldn't you like to bring her to a command performance of a comedy ballet?

MADAME J: Oh yes, we do enjoy a good laugh. It's just what we need.

DORANTE: I think, Madame Jourdain, you were besieged by admirers when you were young. You must have been so pretty and sweet-tempered.

MADAME J: Oh? Then Madame Jourdain is now decrepit and doddering?

DORANTE: Good heavens, I apologize. I forgot that you're still young. I'm so absentminded. Please forgive me.

(enter Jourdain)

JOURDAIN: Here you are: two thousand two hundred francs in hard cash.

DORANTE: I assure you, Monsieur Jourdain, that you can ask anything of me. I'm eager to do you some service at court.

JOURDAIN: I'm very obliged to you.

DORANTE: If Madame Jourdain would like to see the command performance, I will get her the best seats in the house.

MADAME J: Madame Jourdain remains your humble servant, but she's busy with the laundry.

DORANTE: *(aside to Jourdain)* As I told you in my note, I've finally persuaded the lovely countess to come here later today to dine and to watch the ballet.

JOURDAIN: Let's move away a little. You can see the reason.

DORANTE: And not until this morning did I finally persuade her to accept the diamond ring you bought for her.

JOURDAIN: How did she like it?

DORANTE: Loved it. Absolutely loved it. I think its beauty will work wonders for your cause.

JOURDAIN: I pray so.

MADAME J: *(to Nicole)* He glues himself to that count.

DORANTE: I rhapsodized, properly, over the richness of your present and the greatness of your love.

JOURDAIN: Your kindness, sir, is too much for me. I am moved beyond words to see a person of your rank stoop to do what you are doing for me.

DORANTE: Come, sir. Rank does not exist between friends. Wouldn't you do the same for me if the tables were turned?

JOURDAIN: Of course, and with all my heart.

MADAME J: *(to Nicole)* That man makes me throw up.

DORANTE: Personally I'll do anything to help a friend. As soon as you told me of your passion for my friend, the charming countess, you saw how I leaped in to advance your cause.

JOURDAIN: True. I'm amazed at your kindness.

MADAME J: Will he never leave?

NICOLE: They seem very close friends.

DORANTE: You've found the right way to touch her heart. There's nothing pleases women more than having people spend money on them. Your frequent serenades, the daily bouquets, the magnificent fireworks on the lake, and the diamond ring and the spectacular party you are giving today— these all speak more loudly of your love than any words you might say to her.

JOURDAIN: Good breeding excites me. I want to win her, and I don't care what it costs.

MADAME J: They're up to no good. See if you can find out what's going on.

DORANTE: You'll soon have the pleasure of seeing her and the time to enjoy it.

JOURDAIN: Yes, I've arranged for my wife to spend the day with her sister.

DORANTE: That's wise. Your wife would be in the way. I've made all the arrangements with the caterer and rehearsed the ballet. It's my own choreography, and if the performance is as excellent as my concept, I'm sure you . . .

JOURDAIN: *(perceives Nicole is listening)* What are you up to, you impertinent . . . *(to Dorante)* . . . let's get out of here.

(exit Jourdain and Dorante)

NICOLE: There is something going on, Madame. They're talking about some affair, and they want you out of the way.

MADAME J: This isn't the first time I've been suspicious of my husband. I believe he's having an affair. I'm going to do my best to find out who it is. Meanwhile, let's think about my daughter. You know how much Cléonte loves her. He's a man after my own heart—reliable and rich. I'd like to help him marry Lucile.

NICOLE: Oh, I'm really glad you feel that way, Madame, because if you like the master, I like his servant just as much. A double wedding would be like a fairy tale come true.

MADAME J: Find him. Give him this message. Tell him to come here and I'll join him in asking my husband for my daughter's hand.

(exit Madame Jourdain)

NICOLE: I'll fly, Madame. I couldn't have a more pleasing errand. I'm about to make some people very happy. *(enter Cléonte and Covielle)* Ah, here you are. What luck. I am a messenger of joy. I have great news for you . . .

CLÉONTE: Get out, you cheat. No more of your lying words.

NICOLE: Is this the way you . . . ?

CLÉONTE: Go away, I tell you. And tell your faithless mistress she'll never make a fool of Cléonte again. And I trusted her.

NICOLE: What is this craziness? My dear Covielle, what is this all about?

COVIELLE: Your dear Covielle, witch! Out of my sight and leave me in peace. And don't talk to me, and so forth . . .

NICOLE: You too!

COVIELLE: I said, I tell you, out of my sight, I—tell you! Never speak to me again!

NICOLE: *(aside)* My goodness! What's biting them? I'd better tell my mistress about this.

(exit Nicole)

CLÉONTE: Can you believe it? Treating a lover like this—the most faithful and affectionate of lovers?

COVIELLE: It's shameful what they've both done—to both of us.

CLÉONTE: I show a young woman all the ardor and tenderness imaginable. In all the world I love only her. I think only of her. She is my only concern, my only desire, my only joy. I speak only of her. I think only of her. I dream only of her. Only for her do I live and breathe. And here is the reward for my devotion: I pass two days without seeing her, which are to me two desolate centuries. I meet her by accident and my heart is transported, joy shines in my face. I fly to her in an ecstasy. And she, faithless wench, turns her head and walks past me as if she'd never seen me in her life.

COVIELLE: And the same thing happened to me.

CLÉONTE: Is there anything, Covielle, to match the deceit of this ungrateful Lucile?

COVIELLE: Or of that Jezebel, Nicole?

CLÉONTE: After all my sacrifices, all the sighs, all the testimonies to her charms . . .

COVIELLE: After all the help I've been in the kitchen . . .

CLÉONTE: All the tears I've shed at her feet . . .

COVIELLE: The buckets of water I've pulled from her well . . .

CLÉONTE: All the warmth I've shown . . .

COVIELLE: All the heat I endured in turning her spit . . .

CLÉONTE: After all that she contemptuously ignores me . . .

COVIELLE: She haughtily turns her back on me.

CLÉONTE: It's treachery.

COVIELLE: It's high treason—deserves flogging.

CLÉONTE: Never, please, think of defending her.

COVIELLE: Heaven forbid.

CLÉONTE: In fact, I'd like you to point out all the defects you see in her.

COVIELLE: Well, I see nothing out of the ordinary about her. She's an affected little minx, a strange specimen for you to fall in love with. You can find a hundred worthier women to fall in love with. To begin with, her eyes are too small.

CLÉONTE: True. Her eyes may be small—but they are full of fire, the most sparkling, most honest, most tender eyes in the world.

COVIELLE: She has a big mouth, huge in fact.

CLÉONTE: Yes, but it is more graceful than other mouths. The sight of that mouth is arousing. It's the most winning, loveliest mouth in the world.

COVIELLE: She's a trifle short.

CLÉONTE: Yes, but graceful and well proportioned.

COVIELLE: She speaks and behaves carelessly.

CLÉONTE: But she is so charming and engaging that she wins all hearts.

COVIELLE: As for wit . . .

CLÉONTE: Ah! That she has, Covielle, subtle and delicate.

COVIELLE: Her conversation . . .

CLÉONTE: . . . is charming.

COVIELLE: She is always serious.

CLÉONTE: Is there anything more tiresome than those women who giggle perpetually?

COVIELLE: But she is more changeable than Eve herself.

CLÉONTE: Yes, that suits a beautiful woman. We must accept that.

COVIELLE: Sir, even a fool can see you'll always love her.

CLÉONTE: I? I'd rather die. I'm ready to hate her as much as I loved her.

COVIELLE: How can you hate her if she's so perfect?

CLÉONTE: Exactly why my revenge will be so brilliant. I resolve to hate her even though she is the most beautiful, attractive, charming, lovely *(enter Lucile and Nicole)* . . . woman I ever . . .

NICOLE: *(to Lucile)* . . . I was completely shocked by it.

LUCILE: It can only be what I told you, Nicole.

CLÉONTE: I won't even speak to her.

COVIELLE: Me too.

LUCILE: What is it Cléonte? Something wrong?

NICOLE: And what's eating you, Covielle?

LUCILE: What's troubling you?

NICOLE: Why the sulking?

LUCILE: Are you a mute, Cléonte?

NICOLE: Has the cat got your tongue, Covielle?

CLÉONTE: *(to Covielle)* Shameless!

COVIELLE: Like Judas.

LUCILE: *(to Cléonte)* I see this morning's meeting has put your nose out of joint.

CLÉONTE: *(to Covielle)* Ah ha! She knows what she's done.

NICOLE: It's our behavior this morning that got your goat.

COVIELLE: They know where the shoe pinches.

LUCILE: It's true, isn't it, Cléonte, that's the reason for your bad temper?

CLÉONTE: Yes, traitor, since I must speak, it is. And let me tell you, you're not going to enjoy your treachery. I will break with you first, before you can have the pleasure of driving me away. Oh, it will be hard to conquer my love for you. It will pain me for a while, I'll suffer, but I'll overcome it, and I'd rather thrust a dagger through my heart than be so weak as to come crawling back to you.

COVIELLE: Ditto for me.

LUCILE: This is much ado about nothing, Cléonte. I'll tell you why I avoided you this morning.

CLÉONTE: *(turning his back)* I don't want to hear.

NICOLE: *(to Covielle)* The reason we passed you by that way . . .

COVIELLE: *(turning away)* I don't want to hear too.

LUCILE: You see, this morning . . .

CLÉONTE: *(walking away)* I said no . . .

NICOLE: *(following Covielle)* Let me just say . . .

COVIELLE: No, you two-timer.

LUCILE: *(following Cléonte)* Listen . . .

CLÉONTE: There's no use talking.

NICOLE: Let me tell you . . .

COVIELLE: I'm deaf.

LUCILE: Cléonte!

CLÉONTE: No!

NICOLE: Covielle!

COVIELLE: No!

LUCILE: Wait!

CLÉONTE: Nonsense!

NICOLE: Listen!

COVIELLE: Forget it!

LUCILE: For a minute!

CLÉONTE: Not for a second!

NICOLE: Wait!

COVIELLE: Never!

LUCILE: Two words!

CLÉONTE: No, it's over!

NICOLE: One word!

COVIELLE: I want nothing to do with you.

LUCILE: *(stopping)* Very well. Since you won't listen to me, go and do as you please.

NICOLE: *(stopping)* If that's the way you behave, think whatever you like.

(now the men start following the women)

CLÉONTE: Well, let's hear the reason for your fine behavior.

LUCILE: I don't feel like telling you now.

COVIELLE: Go on, tell us your story.

NICOLE: You won't hear it from me.

CLÉONTE: Tell me . . .

LUCILE: Not a word.

COVIELLE: Let's hear the story.

NICOLE: No story.

CLÉONTE: Please!

LUCILE: I said no!

COVIELLE: I beg you!

NICOLE: Leave me alone!

CLÉONTE: Lucile!

LUCILE: No!

COVIELLE: Nicole!

NICOLE: Never.

CLÉONTE: In heaven's name!

LUCILE: I will not!

COVIELLE: At least speak to me!

NICOLE: No!

CLÉONTE: Clear up my doubts!

LUCILE: I'll do nothing of the kind.

COVIELLE: Ease my mind.

NICOLE: I don't feel like it.

CLÉONTE: Very well. You refuse to ease my suffering by explaining the unseemly way you've treated my love. Look at me for the last time. I go far away to die of grief and love.

COVIELLE: And I am right behind him

(the men turn to go)

LUCILE: Cléonte!

NICOLE: Covielle!

(the men stop)

CLÉONTE: Eh?

COVIELLE: What is it?

LUCILE: Where are you going?

CLÉONTE: Where I told you.

COVIELLE: We're going to die.

LUCILE: To die, Cléonte?

CLÉONTE: Yes, since you so cruelly wish it.

LUCILE: I? I wish you to die?

CLÉONTE: Yes, you do.

LUCILE: Who told you that?

CLÉONTE: Isn't that the case when you refuse to clear up my suspicions?

LUCILE: Is that my fault? If you had only listened to me, you would have found our action was caused by the presence of my old aunt. She's convinced that the mere approach of a man is enough to dishonor a woman. She lectures us constantly that all men are devils to be avoided at all costs.

NICOLE: That is the whole story.

CLÉONTE: That's the truth, Lucile?

COVIELLE: It's not a trick, is it?

LUCILE: It's absolutely true.

NICOLE: That's just the way it is.

COVIELLE: Do we fall for this?

CLÉONTE: Ah! Lucile. How one word from your beautiful, luscious mouth brings peace to my heart.

COVIELLE: How easily we're hooked by these little devils.

(They all embrace. Enter Madame Jourdain.)

MADAME J: I'm very glad to see you, Cléonte. You're here in the nick of time. My husband is coming; this is your chance to ask him for Lucile's hand.

CLÉONTE: What sweet words. It is a most welcome order. *(enter Jourdain)* Sir, I have a request, one that I have long thought about, over a considerable period of time. Sir, I ask you to give me the honor of being your son-in-law.

JOURDAIN: Before I answer I must ask you a question: are you a gentleman born?

CLÉONTE: Sir, most people would not hesitate to apply that word to themselves. It is easily said and easily claimed. I have other views on the subject. I think it is unworthy to steal a title and pass oneself off for what one is not. My family has long held honorable office. I spent six meritorious years in the army, and I am wealthy enough to maintain a respectable position in society. Still, I'm unwilling to call myself what others in my place would not hesitate to claim as their right. Sir, I will tell you frankly, I am not a gentleman by birth.

JOURDAIN: On your way then, sir. My daughter's not for you.

CLÉONTE: What?

JOURDAIN: You are not a gentleman. You can't have her.

MADAME J: What is this gentleman business? Are we descended from Saint Louis?

JOURDAIN: Quiet, wife! I know what you're doing.

MADAME J: Didn't we both come from a line of good, honest tradesmen?

JOURDAIN: Hogwash.

MADAME J: And wasn't your father a shopkeeper, just like mine?

JOURDAIN: Damn that woman! She'll never stop bringing that up. If your father was a shopkeeper, so much the worse for him. As for mine, only the ignorant say that. For the last time, I'm telling you that I want a son-in-law who is a gentleman.

MADAME J: Your daughter needs a husband who suits her. She's much better off with an honorable man who is rich and handsome than some ugly fop of a gentleman without a penny.

NICOLE: She's right! The son of our village squire is the ugliest moron you've ever seen.

JOURDAIN: Shut up, Miss Insolent. You're always sticking your nose in the conversation. I have riches enough for my daughter. All she needs is a coat of arms. I will make her a countess.

MADAME J: A countess?

JOURDAIN: Yes, a countess.

MADAME J: Heaven help us.

JOURDAIN: I've made up my mind.

MADAME J: Well, unmake it. Marrying above one's station leads to double trouble. I don't want a son-in-law who criticizes my daughter for her parents, and I don't want her children to be ashamed to call me grandma. If she should come to visit me in her fancy carriage and, by mistake, doesn't say hello to one of our neighbors, you can imagine what they'd say: "Look at that show-off. She's Monsieur Jourdain's daughter, and when she was little we were good enough for her. She wasn't so high and mighty then. Both her grandfathers were in the dry-goods business. They piled up a lot of money for their children. But you don't get so rich by being honest." Well, I don't want this cackling. I want a man who will be grateful to me for my daughter, to whom I can say, "Sit down there, son-in-law, and have dinner with me."

JOURDAIN: These are the petty views of a narrow mind. Well, you can stay downtrodden forever. My daughter will be a countess in spite of everyone, and if you keep yammering on and get me angry enough I'll make her a duchess.

(exit Jourdain)

MADAME J: Cléonte, don't give up yet. Lucile, come with me and tell your father, straight out, that if you can't have him you'll never marry.

(exit Madame Jourdain, Lucile, and Nicole)

COVIELLE: Well, your high moral principles really did it.

CLÉONTE: What else could I do? I believe in those principles even if others don't.

COVIELLE: Well, he's one that don't. Don't you see he's obsessed? Would it have cost you anything to go along with his fantasies?

CLÉONTE: You're right. But I didn't think it necessary to submit proofs of nobility to become Monsieur Jourdain's son-in-law.

(Covielle starts to laugh)

CLÉONTE: What's so funny?

COVIELLE: I just had an idea.

CLÉONTE: For what?

COVIELLE: For getting you married to your short, big-mouthed sweetheart and tricking old Jourdain at the same time. Oh, I am a genius. Let's go. I've got to get you ready.

(Exit Cléonte and Covielle. Enter Jourdain. A servant enters.)

SERVANT: Sir, the count is here, with a lady.

JOURDAIN: Good God! I have orders to give. Tell them I'll be here right away.

(Exit Jourdain. Enter Dorante and Dorimène.)

SERVANT: The master will be here presently.

(exit servant)

DORANTE: Very well.

DORIMÈNE: I don't know, Dorante. I am letting you bring me to a house where I don't know anyone. It's strange.

DORANTE: Where else, Madame, can I take you to show my love since, to avoid gossip, you won't agree to either your house or mine?

DORIMÈNE: Yes, but what you're not saying is that little by little I'm being drawn in to accept your love. I try to refuse, but you wear me down with a polite obstinacy which I can't keep denying. First the frequent visits, then impassioned declarations accompanied by serenades, parties, and finally rich gifts. I tried to resist it all, but you're not to be discouraged and my resolutions are slowly crumbling. Really, I'm no longer sure of myself, and I think, in the end, you will drag me into marriage in spite of myself.

DORANTE: Indeed, Madame, you ought to have been brought to it before. You are a widow of independent means obligated to no one but yourself. I'm my own master, and I love you more than life. What keeps you from making me the happiest of men—today?

DORIMÈNE: Truthfully, Dorante, it takes many good qualities on both sides for a happy, married life.

63

And even the most reasonable people have trouble finding satisfaction in marriage.

DORANTE: You exaggerate, my dear, in imagining so many difficulties. You shouldn't draw universal conclusions from one unfortunate experience.

DORIMÈNE: Anyway, I come back to this point: your lavish presents disturb me for two reasons—one, they obligate me more than I wish, and two, if I may say it, it must be financially difficult for you, and I don't want that.

DORANTE: Ah, Madame, these are mere trifles. They are not meant to . . .

DORIMÈNE: I know what I'm talking about. For instance, this great diamond . . .

DORANTE: Oh, Madame, please! To me your worth is far greater than the value of such trinkets. I ask you . . . but here, unfortunately, comes our host.

(Enter Jourdain. He makes two sweeping bows and finds himself too close to Dorimène.)

JOURDAIN: Step back a little, Madame.

DORIMÈNE: What?

JOURDAIN: One step back, please.

DORIMÈNE: What for?

JOURDAIN: Just a little back, for the third bow.

DORANTE: Monsieur Jourdain knows his etiquette.

JOURDAIN: Madame, it is a matter of great pride to me to be so fortunate as to be so happy as to have the happiness that you had the kindness to grant me the grace of doing me the honor of honoring me with the favor of your presence: and if I had the worth to be worthy of such worth as yours, and if heaven . . . envious of my happiness . . . had granted me . . . the advantage of finding myself worthy . . . of the . . .

DORANTE: Monsieur Jourdain, enough. Madame doesn't care for great compliments, and she knows that you are clever and witty. *(aside to Dorimène)* He is a worthy citizen if a bit ridiculous, as you see, in his behavior.

DORIMÈNE: *(aside to Dorante)* That's not hard to see.

DORANTE: Madame, this is my dearest friend.

JOURDAIN: You do me too much honor.

DORANTE: A gallant man.

DORIMÈNE: Then I have great respect for him.

JOURDAIN: I've done nothing yet, Madame, to deserve such a favor.

DORANTE: *(aside to Jourdain)* Be sure not to mention the diamond you gave her.

JOURDAIN: Couldn't I even ask her how she likes it?

DORANTE: What? Absolutely not! It would be totally vulgar. As a true gentleman you must act as if you know nothing about it. *(to Dorimène)* Monsieur Jourdain says he is delighted to see you in his house.

DORIMÈNE: He honors me greatly.

JOURDAIN: *(aside to Dorante)* How obliged I am to you for saying those things about me.

DORANTE: I had the devil of a time getting her to come here.

JOURDAIN: I don't know how to thank you.

DORANTE: Madame, he says he thinks you are the most beautiful woman in the world.

DORIMÈNE: That's very kind of him.

JOURDAIN: Madame, it is you who are kind and . . .

DORANTE: Let's think about dinner.

(enter a servant)

SERVANT: Dinner is ready, sir.

DORANTE: Let's sit down then; and send in the musicians.

[Ballet. Six cooks enter. They bring in a table covered with dishes. The guests act out their various relationships, the diamond is shown and admired. Two male singers, a woman singer, and several servants remain on stage.]

COOK'S SONG: My kitchen's a kingdom
And I am its king.
Great meals are my subject,
Great food is my thing.

My favorite recipe
From heaven above,
Good wine and good food
And the prospect of love.

But never forget,
In your tireless quest,
To complement food
Takes a most charming guest.

DORIMÈNE: Really, Dorante, this is a magnificent dinner.

JOURDAIN: It's kind of you to say that, Madame. I wish it were more worthy of your favor.

DORANTE: Monsieur Jourdain here is quite right. Although I am grateful to him for so favoring us in his house, I agree with him that this feast is unworthy of you. Since I ordered it, and since I don't have the competence in these matters of some of our friends, you will not rate this a great gourmet experience, and you will perhaps notice some culinary lapses, some barbarism of taste. If our great chef, Damis, had had a hand in it, all would be according to rule, abounding in elegance and erudition. He would eagerly call to your attention the excellence of the dishes served. He would ask you to acknowledge his skill in the art of cooking. He would make mention of the bread, crusty and golden brown, yielding tenderly to the tooth. He would tell us of a velvety wine, tangy but not overpoweringly so, of a shoulder of mutton seasoned with parsley, of a loin of veal from the meadows of Normandy, white, tender, and like almond paste on the tongue, of partridges in a sauce of matchless flavor, and for his masterpiece, a young, fat turkey flanked by squabs, crowned with white onions blended with endive. But for my part I must admit my culinary ignorance and, as Monsieur Jourdain has very well said, I wish the feast were more worthy of your acceptance.

DORIMÈNE: I can only answer this compliment by eating this fine dinner.

JOURDAIN: Oh, what beautiful hands!

DORIMÈNE: The hands are ordinary, Monsieur Jourdain, you must mean the diamond, which is indeed beautiful.

JOURDAIN: Diamond? God forbid that I should mention it. That would not be gentlemanly. The diamond is a mere trifle.

DORIMÈNE: You are hard to please.

JOURDAIN: You are too kind . . .

DORANTE: *(cautioning Jourdain with a sign)* Come, some wine for Monsieur Jourdain and for our musicians, who will now do us the favor of singing a drinking song.

DORIMÈNE: It is wonderful to accompany good food with good music. I am being royally entertained here.

JOURDAIN: Madame, no more than is your due . . .

DORANTE: Monsieur Jourdain, let's listen to the musicians. They will express with notes more than we can with words.

(the singers raise their glasses and sing)

SINGER: Phyllis, love, please fill my glass.
You lend the wine an extra charm.
I love you both my fair, sweet lass.
You and wine can do no harm.

Away with doubt, love while you can.
Your lips will drive away all care.
Wine a woman and a man.
Eternal love we'll swear.

DORIMÈNE: I've never heard better singing. Beautiful.

JOURDAIN: I am looking at something even more beautiful.

DORIMÈNE: Why, Monsieur Jourdain is more of a diplomat than I thought.

DORANTE: Why, Madame, what did you take him for?

JOURDAIN: I could suggest something she could take me for.

DORIMÈNE: You won't stop?

DORANTE: You don't know him yet.

JOURDAIN: She can know me better whenever she wants to.

DORIMÈNE: Oh, I give up.

DORANTE: He always has an answer. Have you noticed, Madame, that Monsieur Jourdain eats all the pieces you've left behind?

DORIMÈNE: I find Monsieur Jourdain to be a charming man.

JOURDAIN: If I could charm your heart I would be . . .

(enter Madame Jourdain)

MADAME J: Well, well. Company. And somehow I wasn't invited. It was for this pretty business, dear husband, that you were so anxious to pack me off to my sister's. Downstairs I see a stage and up here a feast worthy of a wedding. So this is how you spend your money: courting the ladies, with me out of the way. They get music and a play, I get my sister. And how much did this all cost?

DORANTE: Madame Jourdain, it's utter nonsense to think your husband is spending his own money and that he's giving this party for the lady. I am paying the bill. Let me tell you that he has only lent us his house. You ought to be a little more careful about what you say.

JOURDAIN: Yes, utter nonsense. It is the count who is giving this for the lady who happens to be a lady of rank. He honors me by borrowing my house and my orchestra and asking me to join him.

MADAME J: Stuff and nonsense. I can see what's going on.

DORANTE: Madame Jourdain, you need a new pair of spectacles.

MADAME J: Sir, I don't need spectacles to see clearly. I've known what's going on for quite a while now. I'm no fool. It is beneath a great lord like you to encourage my husband in his idiot fantasies. And for a great lady like you, Madame, it is neither seemly nor honest for you to be a home-wrecker, allowing my clueless husband to fall in love with you and not putting him in his place.

DORIMÈNE: What is this bizarre creature saying? Dorante, does it amuse you to see me abused by this weird woman? If so, you can enjoy the joke without me. *(she storms out)*

DORANTE: *(following)* Madame, wait! Where are you going?

JOURDAIN: Madame ... My Lord, apologize to her and try to bring her back. *(Exit Dorante. To Madame J:)* Damned troublemaker! A very nice day's work. You insult me in front of everybody and drive people of quality out of my house.

MADAME J: Stuff their quality.

JOURDAIN: I am close, very close to crowning you with the leftover of this fabulous meal—which you have now completely ruined.

(the servants carry out the table)

MADAME J: *(snaps her fingers)* This for your threats. I'm defending my rights. Every wife in the world would be on my side. *(leaving)*

JOURDAIN: That's right. Run away before I lose control.

(she exits)

JOURDAIN: Damn! She came at just the wrong time. I was just at the point of saying some great things. I never felt so inspired. *(enter Covielle in disguise)* Who the hell are you?

COVIELLE: Sir, I don't think I have the honor of being known to you.

JOURDAIN: Damn right.

COVIELLE: *(holding his hand a foot from the floor)* The last time I saw you, you were this tall.

JOURDAIN: I was?

COVIELLE: Yes. You were the prettiest child in the world. All the ladies would take you in their arms to kiss you.

JOURDAIN: To kiss me?

COVIELLE: Yes. You know, I was a great friend of your late esteemed father.

JOURDAIN: My late esteemed father?

COVIELLE: Yes, he was a very worthy nobleman.

JOURDAIN: What did you say?

COVIELLE: I said he was a very worthy nobleman.

JOURDAIN: My father?

COVIELLE: Your father.

JOURDAIN: You knew him well?

COVIELLE: Very well indeed.

JOURDAIN: And you knew him to be a nobleman?

COVIELLE: Without a doubt.

JOURDAIN: Then I don't understand what's going on.

COVIELLE: What do you mean?

JOURDAIN: There are some stupid people who tell me he was a shopkeeper.

COVIELLE: He, a shopkeeper? It's pure slander. The truth is since he was very kind and helpful and a remarkable judge of cloth, he went here and there choosing strips for his collection. He would then give them to his friends—for money.

JOURDAIN: I'm delighted to know you and to hear from you that my father was a nobleman. I am most obliged to you. And what business brings you here?

COVIELLE: Since the time I had the privilege of knowing your late father, I have been traveling this wide world.

JOURDAIN: The whole world?

COVIELLE: Yes.

JOURDAIN: That must be a long trip.

COVIELLE: A very long trip. I returned from my extensive travels just four days ago, and since I am interested in everything that concerns you, I have come to bring very good news.

JOURDAIN: What is that?

COVIELLE: You know, of course, that the son of the Turkish sultan is here?

JOURDAIN: Me? No.

COVIELLE: Really. Where have you been? He has an absolutely magnificent retinue. Everyone flocks to see him, and he has been received here as a very important nobleman.

JOURDAIN: My goodness! I didn't know that.

COVIELLE: The advantage to you in all this is that he's in love with your daughter.

JOURDAIN: The son of the Turkish sultan?

COVIELLE: Yes, and he wants to be your son-in-law.

JOURDAIN: My son-in-law? The son of the Turkish sultan?

COVIELLE: You've got it. The son of the Turkish sultan hopes to be your son-in-law. Do you speak Turkish?

JOURDAIN: No.

COVIELLE: When I visited with him, he said to me, after we discussed various matters—I understand his language perfectly—"*Acciam croc soler ouch alla moustaph gidelum varahini oussere carbulath.*" That is to say, "Have you, perhaps, seen a beautiful young lady, the daughter of Monsieur Jourdain, a Parisian nobleman?"

JOURDAIN: The son of the Turkish sultan said that about me?

COVIELLE: Those were his very words. When I told him I knew you very well and that I had seen your daughter, he said, "*Ah, marababa sahem,*" which means "I am deeply in love with her."

JOURDAIN: "*Marababa sahem*" means "I am deeply in love with her"?

COVIELLE: Yes.

JOURDAIN: Oh, how I love language. I never would have thought that "*marababa sahem*" could mean "I am deeply in love with her." This Turkish is a wonderful language.

COVIELLE: More wonderful than you can imagine. Do you know what "*cacaracamouchen*" means?

JOURDAIN: "*Cacaracamouchen*"? No.

COVIELLE: It means "my darling."

JOURDAIN: "*Cacaracamouchen*" means "my darling"?

COVIELLE: Wonderful accent.

JOURDAIN: This is really marvelous. *Cacaracamouchen*—my darling. Can you imagine? I'm amazed.

COVIELLE: In short, to complete my mission, I must tell you the Turk is coming to ask for your daughter's hand in marriage. And to have a father-in-law worthy of him he proposes making you a

74

mamamouchi, which is a high personage in his country.

JOURDAIN: A *mamamouchi*?

COVIELLE: Yes, a *mamamouchi*, which is, in our language a . . . paladin. Paladin—in ancient times a paladin was . . . well, you know, a paladin. There's nothing more noble on earth.

JOURDAIN: The son of the Turkish sultan honors me profoundly. Please take me to him so I can express my thanks personally.

COVIELLE: That's not necessary. He's coming here.

JOURDAIN: He's coming here?

COVIELLE: Yes, and he's bringing everything necessary for your investiture.

JOURDAIN: He works very fast.

COVIELLE: He is deeply in love.

JOURDAIN: There's one troubling thing. My daughter is as stubborn as an English mule. She's determined to marry a certain Cléonte, and she swears she'll marry no one else.

COVIELLE: She'll change her mind when she sees the son of the Turkish sultan. Besides, it's a remarkable fact that the son of the Turkish sultan bears a striking resemblance to Cléonte. I just had him pointed out to me. The love she feels for the one can easily transfer to the other and . . . ah, here he is.

(Music. Enter Cléonte ridiculously disguised as a Turk. Three pages carry his long train.)

75

CLÉONTE: *Ambousahim oqui boraf, Giourdina salmala-qui!*

COVIELLE: *(translating to Jourdain)* "Monsieur Jordain, may your heart be like a rosebush blooming all year round." This is the polite form of expression in his country.

JOURDAIN: I am your Turkish Highness's humble servant.

COVIELLE: *Carigr camboto oustin moraf.*

CLÉONTE: *Oustin yoc catamalaqui basum base alla moran.*

COVIELLE: He says, "May heaven grant you the strength of a lion and the cunning of a serpent."

JOURDAIN: His Turkish Highness honors more than I deserve, and I wish him lots of good luck.

COVIELLE: *Ossa binamen sadoc babally oracaf ouram.*

CLÉONTE: *Bel-men.*

COVIELLE: He says you must quickly go with him to prepare the investiture ceremony, and afterward to your daughter to conclude the marriage.

JOURDAIN: All that in two words?

COVIELLE: The Turkish language is like that. It says a great deal in a very few words. Go with him at once.

(exit Jourdain, Cléonte, and pages)

COVIELLE: *(laughing)* What a fool. He couldn't have played his part better if it had been written for him. *(enter Dorante)* Sir, I wonder if you would be kind enough to help us out in a little performance that we're staging.

DORANTE: Ah, it's Covielle! I hardly recognized you. What kind of getup is that?

COVIELLE: You noticed. *(laughing)* It's part of a scheme to trick Monsieur Jourdain into marrying Lucile to Cléonte.

DORANTE: I can't guess what it is, but I can guess that it will work if you had a hand in it.

COVIELLE: I can see, sir, that you know the players.

DORANTE: Tell me about it.

COVIELLE: Please step over here to make room for what I see coming in. You will see part of the business while I tell you the rest.

[Ballet. The Turkish ceremony of Jourdain's investiture is performed with music and dance. Six Turks enter, two by two, carrying three long carpets. They flourish them, then raise them on high. The Turkish musicians pass beneath. Four dervishes accompanying the Mufti close the procession. The Turks spread the carpets on the ground and kneel on them. The Mufti, standing in the center, makes an invocation with contortions and grimaces, turning up his face and wiggling his hands outward from his head like wings. The Turks touch their foreheads to the floor singing "Ali." They resume kneeling, singing "Allah." They continue this to the end of the ceremony, then they stand, singing "Allah akbar." The dervishes bring Jourdain, in Turkish costume, before the Mufti.]

MUFTI: Mahametta, per Giourdina
Mi pregar sera e mattina
Voler far un paladina
De Giourdina, de Giourdina
Dar turbanta, e dar scarcina
Con galera e brigantina

77

Per deffender Palestina
Mahametta per Giourdina
Mi pregar sera e mattina.

(to the Turks) E Giourdina con Mahametta?

TURKS: Yes, by Allah! Yes he is!

MUFTI: *(dancing and chanting) Allah baba hou. Allah hou!*

(the dervishes place a copy of the Koran on Jourdain's back, and the Mufti reads from it)

MUFTI: *Ti non star furba?*

TURKS: No, no, no. Giourdina no heathen!

MUFTI: *Non star furfanta?*

TURKS: No, no, no. Giourdina no devil.

MUFTI: *Donar turbanta, donar turbanta! (they place an enormous turban on Jourdain's head) Dara dara Bastonnara*

TURKS: *Bastonnara, bastonnara.*

(They give Jourdain a ceremonial beating with their scimitars, then raise him up. Now they do a wild, sensual dance. The rite is over. The Mufti bows to him.)

MUFTI: *Giourdina, Mamamouchi.*

(After the ceremony all retire except Jourdain, who is dazed and happy. Enter Madame Jourdain.)

MADAME J: Lord have mercy on us! He's gone round the bend. You look ridiculous. Is this carnival time? Speak up. What's going on? Who dressed you like that?

JOURDAIN: Impudent woman, speaking like that to a mamamouchi.

MADAME J: A what?

JOURDAIN: Mamamouchi. I tell you I'm a mamamouchi.

MADAME J: What kind of animal is that?

JOURDAIN: Mamamouchi, which in our language
means nobility.

MADAME J: True, you have no ability, and it's a shame
at your age.

JOURDAIN: Pure ignorance. I said nobility. I am a paladin.

MADAME J: You're a . . . ? What's that on your head?

JOURDAIN: Ignorant woman. This is my ceremonial
turban.

MADAME J: What ceremony?

JOURDAIN: *Mahametta per Giourdina.*

MADAME J: What does that mean?

JOURDAIN: Giourdina, that is, Jourdain—me.

MADAME J: What about Jourdain?—you?

JOURDAIN: *Voler far un paladina de Giourdina.*

MADAME J: What?

JOURDAIN: *Per deffender Palestina.*

MADAME J: What is this nonsense?

JOURDAIN: *(singing and dancing)* Hou la ba ba la chou
ba la ba ba la. *(he falls to the ground)*

MADAME J: Oh my God! My husband is going crazy.

JOURDAIN: *(rising and exiting)* Peace, insolent woman.
Show some respect to his lordship, the mamamouchi.

MADAME J: What happened to him? He can't be allowed out like this. *(exit)*

(enter Dorante and Dorimène)

DORANTE: Yes, Madame, you are about to see the funniest sight imaginable. I don't think you'll find a crazier man anywhere. We must support Cléonte by confirming his masquerade. He's a good man who deserves all the help we can give him.

DORIMÈNE: I'm very impressed with him. He deserves to win out.

DORANTE: Besides, we have a ballet coming.

DORIMÈNE: Yes, I saw some enormously lavish preparation going on. Really, Dorante, I can't allow you to go on bankrupting yourself. So to put a stop to all this spending on me I've decided to marry you at once. As you know, after marriage all this sort of thing stops.

DORANTE: Ah, Madame, is that really true?

DORIMÈNE: It's only to keep you from ruining yourself. If I don't do something quickly, you'll have nothing left.

DORANTE: I'm deeply grateful, Madame, for the care you've taken to preserve my property. It's entirely yours and my heart with it. Both of them yours to command.

DORIMÈNE: I shall treat them both with great consideration. Oh, and here's our man now. He certainly does look extraordinary.

(enter Jourdain)

DORANTE: Your Excellency, we have come to pay homage to your new rank and to congratulate you on the marriage of your daughter to the son of the Turkish sultan.

JOURDAIN: *(after making his bows)* Sir, I wish you the strength of serpents and the cunning of lions.

DORIMÈNE: I am delighted to be among the first, sir, to congratulate you on the height of glory to which you have risen.

JOURDAIN: Madame, may your rosebush bloom all year round. I am infinitely obliged to you for the interest you've shown in the honors I've received, and I'm greatly rejoiced that you have returned to my palace so that I can extend my humble apologies for my wife's goddamned excessive behavior.

DORIMÈNE: There's no reason for that. Your love must be very precious to her. It's not strange that having a husband with such talents should cause problems.

JOURDAIN: But Madame, I am entirely yours.

DORANTE: You see, Madame, Monsieur Jourdain isn't one of those people who are dazzled by prosperity. Even in all his glory he remembers his old friends.

DORIMÈNE: That is the mark of a truly noble soul.

DORANTE: Where is his Turkish highness? As your friends, we would like to pay our respects.

JOURDAIN: Here he comes now. I've sent for my daughter to marry him.

(Enter Cléonte in Turkish costume. He holds out his hand for Dorimène to kiss.)

DORANTE: Sir, as friends of your honorable father-in-law, we have come to pay your highness our respects and to assure you of our humble services.

JOURDAIN: Where is the interpreter to tell him who you are and what you are saying? As you'll see, he'll answer you: he speaks Turkish beautifully. Hello! Where in hell has he gone? *(to Cléonte)* *Strouf, strif, strof, steaf.* This gentleman is a *grande segnore, grande segnore. Grande Segnore;* and the lady is a *grande dama, grand dame. (seeing that he is not understood)* Damn! Oh good! There's the interpreter. *(enter Covielle)* Where have you been? We can't speak a word without you. Just tell him that this lady and gentleman are persons of the highest rank who have come, as my friends, to pay their respects to him and to assure him of their services. Wait till you hear this!

COVIELLE: *Alabala crociam acci boram alabamen.*

CLÉONTE: *Catalequi tubal ourin sate amalouchan.*

JOURDAIN: There, you see? Pure magic.

COVIELLE: He says, "May the rain of prosperity forever water your family's garden."

JOURDAIN: Didn't I tell you he spoke Turkish!

DORANTE: Admirable!

(enter Lucile)

JOURDAIN: Come, my daughter, come here. Come and give your hand to this gentleman who does you the honor of asking to marry you.

LUCILE: Father, look at you! Are you in a play?

JOURDAIN: No, no. This is not a play. This is a very serious matter, one that does you the greatest honor. Here is the husband I am presenting to you.

LUCILE: Husband—to me, father?

JOURDAIN: Yes. To you. Now give him your hand and thank heaven for your good fortune.

LUCILE: I don't want to get married.

JOURDAIN: I want you to, and I'm your father.

LUCILE: I'll do no such thing.

JOURDAIN: What a fuss! Come, I say. Here, your hand.

LUCILE: No, father. I've told you, no power in the world can force me to accept anyone but Cléonte; and I will do anything rather than . . . *(she recognizes Cléonte)* True, you are my father and I owe you my complete obedience, and it is your right to dispose of me in any way you see fit.

JOURDAIN: Ah! I'm delighted you recognize your duty. I like an obedient woman.

(enter Madame Jourdain)

MADAME J: What in the world is going on? I hear you're marrying your daughter to some kind of clown?

JOURDAIN: Will you shut up, woman? You always stick your nose in at the wrong time, and there's no way you'll ever learn.

MADAME J: You're the one who'll never learn anything. You just go from folly to folly. What are you up to now? And what are you trying to do with this crazy marriage?

JOURDAIN: I intend to marry my daughter to the son of the Turkish sultan.

MADAME J: The son of the Turkish sultan!

JOURDAIN: Yes. You may present your compliments to him through that interpreter.

MADAME J: I couldn't care less about any interpreter. I'll tell him myself, to his face, that he's not having my daughter.

JOURDAIN: Once more, will you shut up?

DORANTE: What, Madame Jourdain, you are against an opportunity like this? You refuse his Turkish Highness as a son-in-law?

MADAME J: My dear sir, mind your own business.

DORIMÈNE: It's a great honor that should be accepted.

JOURDAIN: I'm asking you not to meddle in a matter that doesn't concern you.

DORANTE: It is out of friendship to you that we concern ourselves with your welfare.

MADAME J: I'll manage without your friendship.

DORANTE: But your daughter has agreed to her father's request.

JOURDAIN: My daughter agrees to marry a Turk?

DORANTE: Absolutely.

MADAME J: She can forget Cléonte?

DORANTE: Ah well, what will one not do to be a great lady?

84

MADAME J: I'd strangle her with my own hands if she ever pulled a trick like that.

JOURDAIN: Enough of this babbling. I tell you this marriage will happen.

MADAME J: And I tell you it won't happen.

JOURDAIN: Babble, babble, babble.

LUCILE: Mother!

MADAME J: Come, you're a nasty piece of work.

JOURDAIN: You're scolding her because she's obeying me?

MADAME J: Yes, she's as much mine as yours.

COVIELLE: Madame!

MADAME J: Now what have you got to say for yourself?

COVIELLE: Just one word.

MADAME J: I don't want to hear any words out of you.

COVIELLE: *(to Jourdain)* Sir, if she will listen to a word in private, I promise she will agree to your wishes.

MADAME J: I won't agree.

COVIELLE: Just listen to me!

MADAME J: No.

JOURDAIN: Listen to him.

MADAME J: I don't want to listen to him.

JOURDAIN: That's a woman's obstinacy for you. Will it hurt you to hear what he says?

COVIELLE: Just listen to me, then you can do whatever you please.

MADAME J: Well . . . all right. What?

COVIELLE: *(aside to Madame J)* We've been signaling you for more than an hour. Don't you see, all this is designed to fit in with your husband's fantasies. This disguise is a trick, and the son of the Turkish sultan is none other than Cléonte.

MADAME J: Oh!

COVIELLE: And I'm Covielle.

MADAME J: Well, in that case I surrender.

COVIELLE: Now, don't give us away.

MADAME J: *(to Jourdain)* All right, I agree to the marriage.

JOURDAIN: At last, everyone is being reasonable. You wouldn't listen to him. I was sure he would explain to you about the son of the Turkish sultan.

MADAME J: He explained it properly and I'm satisfied. Let's send for the notary.

DORANTE: Good. And Madame Jourdain, just to set your mind at rest in case you were suspicious of your husband, this lady and I shall make use of the same notary for our marriage.

MADAME J: I give my consent to that too.

JOURDAIN: *(aside to Dorante)* That's just to fool her, isn't it?

DORANTE: Just a pretense to divert her suspicions.

JOURDAIN: Good. Good idea. *(aloud)* Send for the notary at once.

COVIELLE: I already have.

MADAME J: What about Nicole?

JOURDAIN: I'll give her to the interpreter and my wife to anyone who'll have her.

COVIELLE: Sir, I thank you. *(aside)* If a greater fool exists I'll take him to Rome and exhibit him to the pope.

[Ballet. The entry of the notary, the marriage of the three couples. Jourdain and Madame Jourdain on stage at the end: he is rueful, she is forgiving. He sees himself in the mirror and bursts out laughing at his new jacket. They embrace.]